PIEBALD

NICOLA DAVIES

Piebald
Published in Great Britain in 2024
by Graffeg Limited.

Written by Nicola Davies copyright © 2024.
Designed and produced by Graffeg Limited copyright
© 2024.

Graffeg Limited, 24 Stradey Park Business Centre,
Mwrwg Road, Llangennech, Llanelli,
Carmarthenshire, SA14 8YP, Wales, UK.
Tel: 01554 824000. www.graffeg.com.

Nicola Davies is hereby identified as the author
of this work in accordance with section 77 of the
Copyright, Designs and Patents Act 1988. 1988.
Welsh translation in Chapter 14 by Gwenno Gwilym.

A CIP Catalogue record for this book is available from
the British Library.

The publisher acknowledges the financial support of
the Books Council of Wales. www.gwales.com.

Printed and bound in Great Britain by Clays Ltd,
Elcograf S.p.A.

ISBN 9781802587494

1 2 3 4 5 6 7 8 9

PIEBALD

NICOLA DAVIES

GRAFFEG

1. Piebald

The horse stood in a narrow strip of waste ground between the bypass and the cemetery wall. How it got there Moxie couldn't work out. The only way into that patch of scrappy grass, brambles and wind-blown rubbish was this gate, but the rusty padlock looked like it had been there since before the dinosaurs were alive.

Moxie's little brother, Ryan, wobbled his way to the gate's top bar to get a better look at the creature. Climbing, like most other skills, was a bit of a stretch for Ry, but he was game, you had to give him that. He took a long look at the horse and delivered his verdict.

'It's mingin',' he said.

Moxie had to agree that Ry had a point. The animal's back was swayed and its head was short. Its hooves splayed out at the bottom of its knobbly legs, like the slippers old men wore to shuffle to the shop for a packet of fags. It looked half-starved and its coat was more mud than fur. But under the mud, Moxie could just make out a patchwork of dark and light.

'Piebald...' The word came out of her mouth before she knew it. *Piebald!* Yes, that's what you called a horse splashed with black and white. But how had she known that? Where had that word come from? Deep in Moxie's mind, a memory stirred, like a fish at the bottom of a pond.

'Piebald,' Ryan said, and grinned. 'Mingin' Piebald!'

'Is that, like, its full name, Ry? Mingin' Piebald?' Moxie laughed. She spoke quietly to the horse. 'You're not minging, just Piebald, aren't you, girl?' Girl? Yes, girl. This was a *mare* – another bit of horse knowledge whose origin Moxie couldn't identify. Weird. She shrugged and dug into the pocket of her tracksuit bottoms for a boiled sweet.

'Hey Ry, d'you wanna feed her?'

She put the sweet in Ryan's hand and stood behind him to stop him from falling. 'Here,' she said, 'do it like this, see? Keep your hand flat.'

She clicked her tongue and Ryan started at the unfamiliar sound. 'That's how you call them, see?' Moxie said. She clicked her tongue again. Ryan did his best to copy, managing a wet sucking sound. He gave up and called out instead.

'Pie-bald! Pie-bald!'

Slowly, as if waking up from sleep, the horse clopped over the dry ground towards them and stopped just short of the gate. It drew back its gristly lips and huffed in its breath, taking in the scent of the humans and the sweet Ryan was holding. It was being cautious. Moxie clicked her tongue again.

'C'mon then, girl,' she said softly. 'C'mon, Piebald.'

The horse tossed its head and the dirty strands of its mane parted, so Moxie could see both its eyes. They were piebald too, one bright brown, the other blue, with lashes pale as toothbrush bristles. The eyes looked at her. Really looked. And Moxie looked back. She had the strangest feeling that she and this horse had met before. But how could that be?

The horse huffed again and stepped closer. Ryan's body trembled now, thrumming with a mixture of excitement and fear. His heart was pounding so hard that Moxie could feel it through his clothes. He held his nerve though, bless him, and glanced round at her, his angel face, little pointed chin, huge eyes lit up like lightbulbs. He smiled, the smile you could power the whole town with.

Ryan went very still. He was holding his breath. Very gently, as if she knew the fear that hid inside the small body before her, the horse placed her nose on his outstretched hand. Still, she didn't take the sweet, she just held out her velvet nose, lightly touching Ryan's palm. The thrill of that touch went right through his body and into Moxie's like a bolt of lightning, shooting her back into her past.

She was Ryan's size again. In sunshine, warm as melted margarine. Her small, round legs stuck out either side of a broad, black and white furry back. Her fingers tangled deep into the scratchy weft of a mane. A voice soft and rasping, wrapped around her.

'A natural, you are. A force of nature!' the voice said. 'I bet you could do anything you set your mind to!' Moxie didn't really understand what being a natural was, but she did understand that being able to do anything was very good indeed. A superpower almost.

The memory was a revelation; the idea that there had been a time when someone believed that she, Moxie, could do *anything, anything she set her mind to* flooded through her and rushed out to meet the present. Moxie noticed the smell of the air, the feel of it on her skin, the green-blue line of the high hills beyond the scrappy little town. She felt all of Ryan's fizzing joy, and all the muddle and hurt of normal life fell away. She knew, for the first time in a long time, that she was actually happy.

Then the chippy van announced its arrival in the cemetery car park with an ear-splitting, plinky-plonk, utterly unrecognisable tune. The horse shied, the sun dipped behind the hills and all the muddy shadows of life leapt up around her once again.

'C'mon then, Ryan,' Moxie sighed. 'Home time.'

Ryan looked at her, considering mutiny, but thought better of it. Instead, he planted wet kisses on his palm, blew them towards the horse and called out to her, 'See ya, Pie-bald!'

2. Daddy's Home

By the time Moxie had hauled Ryan across the cemetery to the gate, Noel Richards and his crew of idiots were milling round the chippy van. They had an old mobile phone and were taking pictures of each other on it. That was one benefit of the satellites going wrong and the internet ending – idiots like Noel Richards couldn't inflict pictures of their arses on the whole world any more. But without its connectivity the phone wasn't that interesting, and the boys were bored, impatient for their chips. There was no hope of slipping past them. As soon as they saw Moxie and Ryan, they started at it.

'Wooo-hoo! Wooo-hoo!'

This was Noel Richard's lame impersonation of a police siren, a sound that wasn't heard much any more. It was his 'trademark' talent. He led the swaggering gang of spotty boys to swarm round, pushing Moxie and her brother back against the outer wall of the cemetery.

'Wooo-hoo! Wooo-hoo!' They were all at it

now.

'Wooo-hoo! Alert! Alert! It's the Broken Bowens!'

The fact that Noel had invented this nickname and thought it clever was yet more evidence of the low quality of the boy's brain. Moxie was sure she could have thought of much better names for a girl with a badly repaired harelip and her 'weird' little fairy-child brother.

Ryan went very quiet and cwtched close, his head burrowing into Moxie's side to blot out the sight of the jeering faces. They were so sure of themselves, these boys, so certain this was going to go the way it always had before: they'd get their fun, and Moxie and Ryan would make it home a little smaller and more afraid than the time before. It made Moxie angry. It had always made her angry, and that's why she'd watched videos in the library on self-defence. The library had been closed for ages now, but Moxie had gone on practising fight moves in front of the mirror. She'd been doing it for ages, but somehow, when Noel and his buddies gathered round, she couldn't make use of what she'd learned. Something in her believed that the Broken Bowens was all that she and Ryan were, or would ever be.

But tonight she felt different. Tonight she was

the girl who could *do anything she set her mind to*. She was *a force of nature, a natural*. She pulled Ryan behind her and stood straight.

'Fuck off, Richards, you moron,' she said. He wasn't expecting that. Moxie saw the flicker of surprise pass behind his eyes. But he was a practised bully and this little show of bravado only gave him a moment's pause before he began again.

'Woooo-hooo, woooo-hooo!' Only this time, more slowly, more full of threat and menace. He leant closer so as to chant right into Moxie's face.

She waited. Waited. Waited. Until he was really, really close, until she could see his pizza face in detail and smell the weed on his breath. Then, she hit him. Not in the face like they do in films – and, anyway, the thought of pimple juice getting on her hand made her gag. No, she hit him in the throat. Fast, the way she'd practised, a precise, surgical blow. He went down like a sack of spuds, before his crew could even work out what had happened.

It had worked! Just like it was supposed to. Like some kind of magic trick. Moxie wanted to stare at her own fist in wonder, but that would be unwise. She grabbed Ryan's arm and pulled.

'Leg it!' she said. 'Now!' Moxie hoped that by

the time Noel had regained enough breath to tell his crew that revenge was the order of the hour they could be almost home, but as they ran through the echoey, piss-smelling tunnel under the bypass, the loud voices behind told Moxie that she hadn't hit Noel anything *like* hard enough. She dodged through the hole in the wall on the side of the old railway buildings, through the ruined ticket office, down the platform, across the tracks and up the other side. But Noel and his boys knew all the nooks and crannies of their broken little town just as well as she did, and Ryan was not a great runner. To be fair, neither was Moxie. As they crossed the waste ground at the back of Mam's house, the gang caught up with them.

It was almost dark now, and the one remaining orange light on their street was coming on. Moxie glanced towards the house, the back garden clogged with dead cars, rusty prams and God only knew how many years of Mam's empty bottles. The windows were all dark. Of course they were, the electricity had been cut off months ago. Even if Mam *was* looking out, what could she do to help? She hardly stepped outside her front door these days. Whatever happened now, they were on their own.

Noel and his boys circled round, not chanting

now, but silent, menacing. Moxie pulled Ryan close and stared them out. Noel held one hand to his throat. He looked terrible. This was bad. Noel's boys wouldn't leave it at a few slaps and scratches – they would do real damage. Right then, there was nothing to lose in that case! Moxie hefted a lump of broken tarmac from the ground and held it up over her head with both arms straight.

'You try to hurt my brother and I'll kill the lot of you!'

The forced laughter didn't come at once. There was a split-second's pause, which told Moxie that although she was backed into a corner, they sensed the danger. Noel tipped his head to the boy next to him. In the distant past, when Moxie had gone to school, this kid had been in her class. Blond and soft back then, he'd been teased for wetting his pants almost every day. Now he pulled a knife and waved it at her.

Moxie lobbed the tarmac and it hit Noel plum in the middle of his chest. He made a kind of '*ooof*' noise and went down. This time he didn't get back up. The boys looked at each other. Who was the leader now? Moxie didn't wait for their decision. With a strength she didn't know she had, she scooped Ryan clear off the ground and ran, screaming at the top of her voice.

Behind her, the gang bellowed their rage and gave chase. She ran on, heart almost bursting, Ryan screaming in her arms. There was a sudden sound of a car engine revving and roaring, becoming instantly deafening; a scrape of blasted gravel, a screech of brakes and blinding headlights, right ahead. Moxie crashed into the bonnet and fell in a heap, tangled up with Ryan. She lay there, panting, trying to stop Ryan clinging on like some kind of demented octopus.

The car door opened, then closed, unhurried. A man stood, silhouetted, facing Noel's crew. Lit up by the headlights, they looked suddenly much smaller.

'So, lads, what's all this about?' The man spoke slowly, seeming calm and collected. He sounded like a teacher or a policeman.

'*She* punched Noel in the throat,' said the blond one. 'That's dangerous, that is.'

'Then she hit him with a rock,' the one next to him added.

'I think she killed him,' a ginger boy added in a strangled splutter, 'the bitch...'

The man held up his hand. 'No language, please, boys,' he said. The boys fell silent. 'Let's get this straight, shall we? You say this *girl* attacked you. But I notice there are quite a *lot* of you and only one of her. And I notice that *you* are carrying a knife.'

As he spoke, he walked slowly towards them, and slightly less slowly, they backed away. 'So I'd suggest, *lads*, that you go off home now, alright? Because if you come near these kids again, you'll be talking to me. OK?'

They nodded. Behind them in the dark, Noel cried out.

'I'd get him to hospital if I was you,' the man added.

The boys held still for a moment, as if they'd been hypnotised. Then they turned and ran.

Still moving slowly, the man walked to where Moxie was fussing over Ryan's scratched arms.

She didn't want to look at the man. What do you say to a person who just saved you? What would they want in return? But the man didn't seem bothered about thanks. He leant his bum against the bonnet of his car and lit a fag.

'So, *did* you hit him in the throat?'

Moxie nodded. The man took a long drag and nodded back.

'Well done!' he said, then he stood up square in front of the two of them. 'Moxie and Ryan, is it?'

Moxie nodded.

'Well then, I'm your Da.'

3. Call Me Dyl

He told them to call him Dyl, not Da or Dad, which was fine by Moxie because Mam had never mentioned any such person. Moxie had assumed that she and Ryan had been the result of a couple of Mam's many 'flings'. Sometimes, back when Mam still had some of her marbles, she would bring a boyfriend home for a few days, so there had been a handful of temporary men in their lives over the years. They had been nothing but trouble, and Moxie had concluded that Mam doing jigsaws at the kitchen table and never going beyond the front door caused a lot less bother than Mam in her high heels going out on the pull.

Anyway, this bloke, Dyl, put them on the back seat of his car and drove them back up the road to get chips from the van. He bought a bag for himself, two each for Moxie and Ryan and whatever drink they wanted. He was already ahead of any other 'Da' they'd known. They sat in the car eating and Moxie examined the man's face in the rearview mirror. Even though he was so old, *forty* probably, he did look a bit like Ryan. The same blue eyes, with the little downward slant at the outer corners, the same dark curls. He was handsome, she guessed, so couldn't be her Da. She thought herself too ugly to have a dad like that.

Stuffed to bursting now, Ryan was dropping off to sleep. Dyl watched him in the rearview mirror. 'What's the matter with him, then?'

Moxie bristled. 'Nothing!' she growled. 'He's tired and he needs his bed.'

'No, c'mon. You know what I mean. Special needs, is it?'

'Like his Da then, I'd say,' Moxie snapped. Whoever this bloke was, he could get stuffed. She wouldn't have anyone talk about Ryan like that. 'Thanks for the chips. Now let us out.' She rattled the handle, but it was locked.

'I'm sorry, alright?' Dyl said. 'I'll take you home, eh?'

There wasn't much of a choice – the door was locked, the car was moving. Moxie sat and seethed. 'Cemetery Street,' she growled at him. 'It's the only house there.'

'Yeah,' he said. 'I know.'

He took them the long way home: around the new estate, abandoned since the last pandemic, where weeds grew from stacks of sand and bricks, and empty windows stared from unfinished walls, then up the high street, where half the houses were empty and all of them looked forgotten. Moxie vaguely remembered when families had lived in most of them, her relatives and friends. Now, only those who couldn't leave remained. It was a town of little old ladies and losers like Noel and his crew, losers like the Broken Bowens.

Dyl wound down his window and looked out. 'There used to be three pubs, a Co-op, a Chinese, an Indian *and* a chippy,' he said. 'There was a barber's on that corner, and a hairdresser's opposite where your Mam worked. There was a bookie too, and a pawn shop.'

How did he know? Was he from around here? She'd never seen him. He took a pull on his fag and blew the smoke out through the window. 'It's dead, this place. All it needs is burying,' he said.

'Why did you come here then?' Moxie snapped.

'To take care of you and your Mam.'

Moxie snorted. His answer sounded like he was reading an advert off a cereal packet. 'Oh yeah, *right!*'

He took another long pull on his fag. 'Alright

then. Have it your own way,' he said. 'I have *business* here. Is that better?'

Moxie looked out of the window at the grand ruins at the top of the high street, buildings whose function no one really remembered now. What business would you do in a town that wanted burying? she wondered.

Dyl threaded the car between the potholes and the landslide that had partly blocked their road years ago. He parked outside the house, neatly, as if it wasn't the only house left standing, the only one spared by the bulldozers that had cleared the way for the bypass.

The engine stopped and the lamp post by the old station cast just enough sickly light to show their ghostly pale faces in the dark car. Moxie caught the keen gleam of the man's eyes in the mirror.

'You got your lip fixed, then?' he said. He was trying to prove that he knew something about her, but anyone could see the way she'd been sewn up. Mam had taken her to a clinic that smelled like the bottom of a bin. Moxie had poked her tongue up her own nose one last time as some bloke with dandruff and a face mask put her to sleep.

'Yeah,' Moxie said, 'when I was eight.'

'Didn't do much of a job, did they?' he said.

Moxie was used to casual cruelty like that. She didn't let it hurt. 'That's why I learned to punch people in the throat,' she said.

Dyl turned in his seat and looked round at her. 'What I mean is, I don't care about your face.' His eyes narrowed, like someone trying to read the instructions of a new appliance written in really small letters. 'I think you are a very capable girl.'

Was she supposed to be flattered?

'Maybe you'd like to help with my business?'

Moxie felt the anger boil up and bubble out like steam. 'Oh really?' she growled. 'And how *helpful* are you going to be to us, then?'

'I just saved you from a beating and bought you chips, didn't I?'

Moxie rolled her eyes at him. 'Thanks, *Da*.'

He shook his head and smiled. He had absolutely perfect teeth. 'OK. OK. Tell me something that I can do, to be *helpful*.'

Ryan opened his eyes and sat up. 'Piebald *food*,' he said. Good old Ry. Spot on again. Moxie almost laughed at the man's confused expression.

'Horse food,' she said. 'You can get us horse food.'

4. Helpful

Moxie had to admit that, so far, Dyl *had* been quite helpful. The house had electricity again, and this time it was free because it arrived in a fat black cable that ran through the kitchen window, not through the meter under the stairs. Moxie and Ryan had beds and there were heaters to keep the bedroom warm. The fridge had food in it, like pizzas and milk. Moxie never saw Dyl bringing the things he got for them. They just appeared, as if a second-hand Santa and his very practical elves had been at work. Dyl himself was mostly absent, although Moxie sometimes spotted his car around town. It was easy to pick it out because not many people had cars any more.

Once in a while he slept in the house, not in Mam's room but on a mattress in the attic. He was usually gone before anyone was up. But not always. Some mornings he would sit at the kitchen table with a cup of coffee while Moxie gave Ryan and Mam their breakfasts. At first he just sat, not saying a word, as if he was trying to be invisible. But gradually he was more and more present. Sometimes he even made the toast and put it on the table. Once, she had been slow getting dressed and heard Ryan screaming in the kitchen. She rushed down to find Dyl wiping Ry's tears with one gentle finger, as if he were touching something made of cloud that would blow away if he breathed on it too hard. He stepped away, embarrassed, as she walked into the room.

'There was a bee,' Dyl mumbled. 'He didn't like it.'

Mam smiled at Dyl sweetly, but she smiled at everyone sweetly these days, it didn't mean anything, really. None of it *meant* anything, Moxie told herself. But all the same, she liked those mornings very much.

As well as the house stuff, Dyl got food for Piebald. They kept a sack of it in the hall and Non helped take a bucketful up to the cemetery every day. Non lived with her 'Two Mams', so called because neither would admit which – Marianne or Judy – was Non's biological mother and they had both brought her up. Marianne was Moxie's mother's older sister, which made Non her cousin. Non was ten years older than Moxie but that didn't matter; the important part was that Non was stuck at home too. Both she and the Mams had experienced what people called 'life-changing injuries' when the train they were travelling on had been blown up by a terrorist bomb. They'd been in London then, but they came home to live after that. The Mams and toddler Non had been more or less stitched back together, but the Mams had been left unable to do much more than sit on the sofa and knit. Non had lost one leg and the other had been mashed up, not good enough to hop about on. So, back in the days when people were given things, Non had been given a *Mobility Vehicle* – a cross between a small greenhouse and an electric scooter that Non called the 'Wagon'. Every afternoon now they drove the Wagon up to the cemetery loaded with a bucket of pony nuts, Ryan on Non's lap so he could drive and Moxie walking alongside. They'd park up amongst the gravestones and sit around chatting while Piebald munched and Ryan cooed over her.

One warm afternoon, while Ryan sat by Piebald and Non leant against a gravestone that announced that Agnes Melania Davies had 'gone into the arms of Jesus', Non said, 'Couldn't get a word out of Two Mams about Dyl.' If anyone would know about Dyl it *should* be Mam's sister and sister-in-law, Moxie thought. 'They *said*,' Non went on, 'that your Mam *never* told them about her boyfriends.'

'Do you think that's true?' Moxie asked.

'Of course not!' Non replied. 'They know something, but they're not saying. You know what they're like. They like keeping secrets. It's a power thing, I reckon.'

If they could keep the secret of Non's true parentage, they could keep quiet about anything. Moxie shrugged. Maybe it didn't matter who Dyl really was if he went on getting them stuff like electricity and pizzas. She sighed and began to work at the rusty padlock with the hacksaw again. It would be much easier to care for Piebald if they could open the gate. Ryan sat on the ground next to the bucket of pony nuts in which Piebald had buried her nose.

'What I *do* wonder, though,' she said, 'is what he's doing *here*. I mean, he seems like a solid sort of bloke. Good-looking, got a car, you know.'

'He is doing right by his beloved children,' Moxie answered.

Non snorted with laughter. 'Don't! There's only so much these incontinence pants will cope with.'

'He said he's got *business* here,' Moxie added.

'Hmm. You watch out, Moxie. There's only

one kind of business going on round here these days, and that's the bad kind. You keep out of it, my girl.'

Non's warning was too late. Moxie was already helping Dyl with his business.

'Do just what you normally do,' he had said. 'Wander about with Ryan.'

Wandering about for Dyl involved deliveries – little parcels that Moxie could fit easily in her backpack with Ryan's drink and snacks. Once in a while, when a police car would turn up and do a couple of circuits of the town, why would they notice a couple of kids not in school? There were kids everywhere not in school these days. In any case, the cops didn't care what happened here. They were soon back on the bypass, whizzing off to somewhere more interesting.

So Moxie and Ryan walked the streets, they sat in the park, on top of walls, they wandered round the backs of houses, just like always. The only difference now was that they knocked on doors and people were pleased to see them. No more taunts from the likes of Noel Richards, now that Moxie was supplying their pills, their weed, their whatever. Oh yes, Moxie knew well enough what Dyl's *business* was, but as Dyl said, 'You know *not to ask*, right, Moxie? A bright girl like you?'

Moxie knew, and she didn't ask when Dyl added a new job to the deliveries either – giving him a list of houses where no one lived, or a house occupied by someone too old to notice noise in their attic. And she didn't ask about the stuff piled up, ready, in the hall. The cables and the light bulbs, the bags of compost and the rolls of stuff like giant tinfoil.

It was clear Dyl's business was going to boom. Already the tin underneath her bed was full of cash. She didn't think about that either, just told herself that it was the Escape Fund, for her and Ryan and maybe Mam as well. But where would she escape to, and when? Well, Moxie didn't think about that either.

The delivering and snooping didn't take up all her time. Moxie could still spend her afternoons with Piebald. She'd finally got through the padlock on the cemetery gate and Dyl had got them a halter so she could lead Piebald with Ryan sitting on her back, and Non in the Wagon at their side. It was lovely to get up the side of the valley to where there were trees. When you looked down on the town the broken bits didn't show so much. But they could never go very far because Moxie and Non had to get back to check on their Mams, and, anyway, the Wagon's battery wasn't brilliant. Moxie sometimes wondered what it would be like to get to the very top, to climb right out of the valley altogether. But mostly she just enjoyed it all: Piebald's slow clop-clop, Ryan's beaming smile, Non's chatter, and spring doing what springs did these days, which was to get warmer and warmer. Life wasn't just muddle and hurt any more – it was good. But it didn't stay that way.

5. Sunny Spells

Mam could just about be trusted to watch Ryan for an hour and make sure he didn't chop his own fingers off or start a fire in the middle of the living room. So at the end of a day that had been eaten up by doing Dyl's jobs and helping old Delyth Thomas pack up her house (she was going to live with her daughter in Leeds), Moxie left her brother in her Mam's care so she could check on Piebald.

Piebald clopped around the cemetery in search of tasty things to eat while Moxie lay down on a gravestone (Thomas Josiah Rees, 1894 – 1981, Safe in God's Keeping). Moxie could talk to her. It didn't matter that she couldn't talk back. When Moxie asked *'So is he really my Da?'* or *'Is he going to go away?'* or *'What happens if he stays?'*, she felt that she had been understood, and that was all that mattered.

Piebald was cleaned up now. She'd filled out, her coat was glossy, her mane was untangled and her eyes shone. But despite her new look, no one came to claim her.

'Where do you come from?' Moxie asked. The horse turned and looked at Moxie as if she really did want to answer this question, and then went right back to grazing. She stripped the grass that had covered a gravestone so old its inscription had worn smooth, but stopped, stock still, her nose touching the edge of the stone. Moxie crouched down next to the pony's nose; there, carved into the side of the gravestone, was the image of a pony, a piebald pony.

Piebald moved on to another grave, worn and ancient as the last, and cropped the grass at its foot to reveal another carving of a horse. Moxie followed as Piebald took a meandering route around the cemetery, stopping, grazing and revealing five more stones with carved ponies. She stopped at last at a much newer stone, shiny and sharp edged, and uncovered another little piebald pony. Like the others, it was carved into the side of the stone, at the bottom, where it might not be noticed, unless you knew what to look for. A secret sign of something that only she knew about. There was no way this was some kind of weird coincidence, was there?

Moxie pinched her own arm to make sure she was awake, then stared at Piebald. 'What do the carvings mean?' she asked, but the horse had already turned her attention back to the bucket with the pony nuts.

Perhaps the most recent stone Piebald had shown Moxie, being newer than the others, would hold some answers. It had fallen on its face and it took all Moxie's strength to raise it up so she could read the inscription; no *'gone into the arms of Jesus'* or *'Safe with the Lord'* or even anything about this person being the *beloved* relative of anyone. There wasn't even a date, just a name, *Florence May Bowen*, and underneath it a single word, *Horsewoman*.

Who had this person who shared her surname been? Had all the others with horses on their gravestones been Bowens too? Did this mean that memory, that lost fragment of her own life in which she had ridden a pony, was true? She wished Piebald could just talk and tell her, but right now it was time to get back – it was getting dark. Moxie put Piebald behind her gate with a new sense of wonder.

Moxie ran down the hill, the bucket clanking at her side and questions battering the inside of her head, but as she took the nettle and dog poo shortcut between the underpass and her house, all those questions went out of her head. A gleaming black car, an SUV so large it looked as if it were designed to hold a different, larger species of human, was parked outside her home. No one in the town had a car like that any more. Almost no one in the country had one. Its fat, sleek luxury said just one thing: trouble.

When she reached the house, someone had left the front door ajar. Moxie slipped inside. There were voices coming from the kitchen, muffled behind the closed door. She slunk into the shadow underneath the stairs and peeked through the crack between the kitchen door and the frame.

Three men in black suits, like people in videos she'd once seen, were there with Mam, Dyl and Ryan. Nobody was smiling. Mam was leaning very close to her jigsaw, as if looking at anything else was just too hard. Dyl was studying the crumbs on the kitchen table. He looked small. They both did, like frightened kids. Only Ryan seemed relatively unfussed about the whole situation. He was playing with a new toy, a yellow digger the size of a loaf of bread. He drove it back and forth over the table, whispering digger noises to himself.

Two of the men were huge, each one the size of an upended sofa, way too big to be standing about in their tiny kitchen. But it was the smaller third one who made Moxie shiver. He was like a large, very life-like doll, with skin stretched pink and smooth, red lips and curly hair, dyed yellow. He sat watching Ryan and the digger, while talking to Dyl.

'So, Dyl, you have really pissed old Sunny Spells right off. Hasn't he, boys?'

Sunny Spells? Was that a real name, Moxie wondered? It seemed it was. The two others nodded then chorused, 'Yeah, right off, Sunny.'

'My plan tonight,' Spells went on, 'was to burn this house and everything in it to the ground. Gotta make an example sometimes, haven't we, boys?'

Once again they nodded and agreed. Dyl just sat there saying nothing, crumb-studying. Spells was still looking at Ryan, as if he was a cake with extra icing. 'Luckily,' he said, 'I like your boy, Ryan. Even prettier than you were yourself at his age.'

Moxie felt the blood drain into her toes and leave her clammy. Sunny Spells showed his white teeth in the sort of smile a snake gives before it swallows a mouse. He reached over the table to snap his fingers right under Mam's nose. She whimpered and drew her face even closer to her jigsaw. 'Shame about the boy's mam, though,' Spells sighed. 'And she was *such* a looker when she was a kid.'

Moxie found her fists were clenched. How she

would like to practise some of her martial arts skills on this bastard. He was still talking. Still smiling. He liked the sound of his own voice. He liked everything about his creepy, horrible self, that was plain enough.

'I've always been fond of this town,' he said. 'It's even better nowadays. No phone signal, almost no cops and a load of losers too desperate to care what goes on. And, as you already know, Dyl, lots of empty houses.' Spells pulled the lists that Moxie had compiled for Dyl from the middle of the table.

'What you *didn't* know,' he continued, 'is that I *already* have business here, up at the old mine. You have inspired me to expand. I'm gonna turn this whole town into my drugs factory. And you, Dyl, are going to help me. Starting tonight.'

He turned to Dyl, who was being lifted from his chair, limp as a scarecrow, by one of the sofa-sized men. 'Don't look so glum, Dyl,' Spells told him. 'I'm just going to show you your new job, after the boys here have reminded you a bit about loyalty.' He smoothed the lapels of his jacket and ran a hand through his golden curls. 'C'mon,' he said. 'Let's go!'

6. The Factory Floor

Moxie only just had time to hide herself behind the boxes stacked under the stairs before the Sofas pushed Dyl through the kitchen door. She waited until the big, black car had growled away and then she went into the kitchen. Mam was hugging Ryan, to his great surprise and not enormous pleasure. 'Get off!' he kept saying. *'Get off!'*

Mam took no notice. Her face was wet with tears. 'Spells!' she said. *'Spells!'*

It was one of the few whole words that Mam had said in months, and she made it sound as if it meant every evil in the world. Mam was clearly terrified of this man. Having seen him and heard him talk, that made perfect sense to Moxie.

There was a lot to unravel here, Moxie reckoned, but for now she knew two things. First, that Mam and Ryan must not stay in the house – Spells might change his mind and come back to burn the place down. Second, that she had to go up to the old mine and find out what this business of Spells' was and what was happening to Dyl. Although he had brought all this down on them, she could imagine what a lesson in loyalty from those two thugs might look like.

Spells and his Sofas couldn't drive directly to the mine from town, as the road had been blocked by the landslide, now overgrown with trees and bushes. So they'd have to go out of town and access the mine from the other side. That still only gave her about half an hour to get Mam and Ryan out of the house and herself up the hill to the complex of ruined mine buildings.

Before she could think about how that would be managed, Mam said, 'Out, out. Marianne. *Non!*' She was definitely having a very good day; two intelligible phrases in as many minutes!

'Yes, Mam. You gotta go to your sister's, to Non's. Get your shoes and I'll get Ryan's stuff, then you can go, OK?'

For a moment Steph stared at Moxie as if she had once again lost the thread of thinking, but then she nodded and rushed upstairs.

'Show Non my digger!' Ryan said, delighted. One of the many things Moxie loved about her little brother was the way he met things, even the most unusual and unexpected, with the greatest optimism. In spite of all that had happened tonight, all he cared about was that he was going to show Non his exciting, new toy.

Astonishingly, in less than ten minutes they were all outside the front door. Ryan with socks, shoes and a bag of jim jams, clean pants and his beloved new digger, and Mam in a relatively normal outfit: metallic boob tube, baggy red tracksuit bottoms, leopard print jacket and white ankle boots. Mam had once delighted in being complimented on her appearance but she took no notice now when Moxie told her she looked nice. She was afraid. She pulled at Moxie's arm. 'Mox!' she said urgently. 'Mox, come.'

'It's OK, Mam, I'll be there very soon, I promise. You go the back way, right? Not down the high street?'

Steph nodded. Moxie hoped she really understood. At this time on a Saturday night the high street was the playground of the likes of Noel Richards with their junk cars, rusty motorbikes and way too many chemicals in their systems. Steph nodded and so did Ryan. Between them Moxie judged they could navigate the way.

The road up to the mine was too steep for running. Moxie panted up it, thinking how men had tramped up and down between the town and the mine for a hundred years, while women washed and cleaned and popped out endless babies. Didn't seem much like fun to Moxie, but perhaps that was better than what had replaced it. She reached the place where the landslide had engulfed the road and began to walk the rough path that led onwards.

It was proper dark up here and Moxie didn't have a torch. There was some gleam from the stars and new moon, but the shadows between the ruined walls of the old mine buildings were so deep that she stumbled about, searching for some kind of clue as to what Spells was up to. She was beginning to wonder if she had taken too long to get here and missed the men's arrival when a car's headlight showed beyond the buildings and she heard the distinctive growl of Spells' SUV. She crouched low and scuttled between the broken walls to get close to where the car had drawn to a stop.

They'd left the headlights on so they shone on the front of the building, which must have been some kind of warehouse back when the mine was in operation. Its windows were tightly boarded up and its roof, unlike those of the other buildings, had been repaired. The entrance to the building was a big metal garage door with massive hinges and three big padlocks. The four men stood in front of it. Well, three of them stood, Dyl was dangling between the two Sofas. In the glare of the headlights, Moxie could see he'd been given a beating.

Moxie was a couple of bus lengths away now, not close enough to hear what was going on. The car was parked between her and the men. If she hid behind it and peeped round she could see *and* hear. The problem was that now she was too afraid to move. Spells and his sidekicks were terrifying. They had threatened to burn her house and her family, and scared both Mam and Dyl witless. What would they do to her if they caught her spying? She should never have come up here, it was beyond stupid!

Spells was close to the door now, bending over to unlock the padlocks. The Sofas were watching him. Now was the moment, nobody would be looking her way, but Moxie was frozen with fear. Then the big metal door swung open and a light, brighter than summer sun, poured out. Moxie shaded her eyes to see. A bright-green mass of tall marijuana plants filled the huge space inside. But that wasn't the shocking thing. There was an inner door made of metal wire, and behind that was a child, dark haired and dark eyed, skinny, dirty and clearly afraid.

It was obvious that this child was a prisoner, kept inside to tend the illegal plants. Moxie had heard of such things, but the reality was so much worse. Her horror overcame her fear. She had to know more. Moxie made her move, but almost at once she stumbled on a stone in the dark. It didn't make much noise, but it was enough. A head turned towards her. She'd been seen.

7. Out of the Box

The Sofas hadn't reacted to the tell-tale crunch of trainer on rock. Nor had Spells. It was Dyl whose head had turned to see her caught in the open. His eyes met Moxie's for the most split of split seconds; he knew the danger she was in and at once he began to struggle and yell. 'Let me go! I don't want any part of this!'

It took all three of his captors by surprise and for five crucial seconds he took all their attention. It was all the distraction Moxie needed to run to the cover of the car. By the time Dyl was subdued, she was crouching by the rear bumper, her heart jumping in her throat. She was close enough now to hear the last punch collide with Dyl's stomach and see him bend double, coughing. She thanked him silently for taking a thrashing to save her skin. The Sofas pulled him upright again and he stood there, swaying.

'That's very disappointing, Dyl,' Spells was telling him. 'You *are* part of this, my boy. You *always* have been. You're *mine*, remember?'

Moxie looked at the kid behind the metal grid. She had backed away from the door and now vanished in between the tall green plants.

'See what you did?' Spells said. 'You frightened the poor little bugger. Boys, get the delivery from the boot. I don't think Dyl will give us any more trouble now.'

The Sofas were returning to the car! To the boot, right where Moxie was! There was only one thing for it – Moxie wriggled under the car and froze again. She squeezed her eyes tight shut. She didn't want to see how close she was to being discovered. She heard the grunts and grumbles as the Sofas lugged stuff out of the boot. Then she heard the clank and bang of the big metal door.

Moxie opened her eyes and peered out. The door was padlocked again. Spells, his thugs and Dyl stood with a pile of black bin bags on the ground beside their feet. Spells kicked one of them with the toe of a shiny leather shoe.

'This is what's needed to finish the job: harvest, process and pack. Your job is to get the supplies inside – there'll be more arriving at your house tomorrow, so you need a little practice now, while I can tell you where you are going wrong.'

'But you locked the door,' Dyl said.

'I did. Because you don't use the front door unless one of the boys is here. I don't want her getting out or you stealing my profits. It goes in up there.' He pointed to a flight of stone steps that ran up the wall beside the metal doors, leading to a small platform at the top. Dyl was still bent over, clutching his punched belly.

'What?' he said. 'Now?'

'Yes, now,' Spells snapped. 'This is staff training, Dyl. Lug this lot up those steps, then I'll tell you what to do.' Dyl groaned and swore as he worked. Spells and his 'boys' thought this was very funny. They shouted instructions up to him.

'Careful with those boxes. Lightbulbs, those are. Use the rope up there to lower them in.'

At last, Dyl staggered back down the steps. He looked terrible. 'That kid,' he coughed, 'where did she come from?'

'She's imported goods. They all are. I buy them small and use them in my growing facilities. When they get bigger, I sell them on to other businesses. I've got a consignment of small ones coming in on Wednesday night and you'll be here to help out and get them to work.'

Spells talked as if he were speaking about some sort of electrical appliance.

'I won't do it, Sunny!' Dyl said. 'They're *kids*!'

'You *will* do it, Dyl. *And* you'll see to establishing more growing houses for me in all those empty properties you found. Don't tell me that wasn't what you were going to do yourself.'

'But I wasn't going to use *kids like slaves*!'

'Haven't *you* become a saint all of sudden! Prison do that for you, did it, Dyl?'

'I won't do it, Sunny. I won't.'

'You certainly will, because I'm going to take little Ryan into protective custody. He's such a *beautiful* boy. I might even keep him. So you had better not put a foot wrong.'

Dyl looked really small now, not at all like the man who'd chased off Noel's gang. Small and broken. He sobbed.

'Oh, get him in the car boys, for God's sake,' Spells snarled. 'Always was a bloody cry baby, as I recall!'

They shoved Dyl into the car and got in so smartly that there was no time for Moxie to get out from under it. As it began to move, she rolled sideways to avoid the swerving back wheels, then lay like a log as the dark swallowed her and the tail lights vanished up the hill.

She scrambled to her feet, heart still pounding, brain fizzing with all she had heard and seen. She had to get to Ryan before they did.

It would take her ten minutes to run down the hill from here. It would take them half an hour, plus however long it would take them to find him. Hours, or maybe even days if they didn't know where to look. That meant she had time to do one last thing before she left. Moxie ran up the stone steps and found the metal hatch cover with the handle. It worked like the big recycling bins there used to be in the car park; you pulled the handle and out came a sort of drawer that you put stuff in, then you closed the handle and the stuff dropped into the bin on the other side. Whether the drawer was open or closed, there was no way for what was inside to get out.

Unless you half-opened it so there was a little gap; unless you had a rope that a person could climb up. Moxie picked up the rope that Spells had advised Dyl to use to lower fragile stuff to the floor below. One end was tied off to a winch beside the metal hatch. Moxie opened the hatch. If she leaned over awkwardly she could see inside to the bright light of the growing space. She dangled the rope through, then called, 'Hello! Hello there!'

Nothing. Damn it. She couldn't take long doing this.

She called again, and this time a small, scared face looked up through the gap.

'I'm going get you out,' she told the child. 'Tie the rope around you and I'll pull you up.'

The child didn't seem to understand, so Moxie mimed tying the rope and pulling. The child grinned – a smile with all the sunshine that Ryan's smile contained. She grabbed the rope and did what Moxie thought was a pretty expert job of tying it around her middle.

Moxie turned the handle on the winch, and the child squeaked and screamed as she was lifted up. It was hard to turn the handle and hold the hatch half-open at the same time, but at last the child dangled next to the hatch. But the gap was too narrow. Not even this small body would fit through.

Moxie saw the solution in a flash, but with their limited store of shared words it would take too long to explain. She shut the hatch, yanked with one last frenzied burst of effort on the winch until the child's body thudded against its drawer-like underside, and then she pulled the hatch open and released the tension on the rope. The child tumbled out onto the concrete. She was dazed and frightened but she seemed to understand that she'd been freed. She stood up and pointed to herself.

'Kuhyen,' she said, 'me name Kuhyen.'

8. Back Story

It began to drizzle, the first rain in weeks. Kuhyen shivered. Moxie gave the little girl her hoodie. It came almost to her ankles, making her look like a miniature Yoda. They ran down the hill, side by side. Kuhyen was quiet, but she didn't seem distressed. Just glad to be out of that horrible place, Moxie guessed. But she did need some kind of explanation about what was going on. Moxie decided to keep it simple: 'You, me and my brother, we run from bad men.' The girl nodded solemnly. She understood about 'running' and 'bad men'.

Moxie threaded a path through all the hidden spaces that she knew so well to the back of the house Non shared with the Two Mams. She pushed the rusted gate open and knocked on the side door. Non opened it at once.

'Oh, Moxie Bowen. Thank God,' she said. 'I got no sense at all out of Ryan or your Mam. She kept saying some name, but the Mams shut her up. I think they're bonkers, all three of them.'

Non led them into the back room. There was a sofa on one wall and a table covered with the bits of old phones and computers that Non loved fiddling with. An old DVD was playing on the ancient telly that Non had repaired a gazillion times. Ryan was fast asleep on the floor, he and his digger wrapped in a blanket. Marianne and Judy were asleep too, slumped together on the sofa like bookends. Steph was in an armchair and got up as they came into the room.

'Mox!' she said. 'Mox!' and gave Moxie a hug like the one she'd given Ryan earlier. She hadn't done that in a long time and it seemed to embarrass her. She sat back in her armchair and studied the floor. Non clicked the DVD off and the two Mams woke up.

'Hello, Moxie,' they greeted her.

'Hello, Mams,' she said back.

Everybody looked at the kid standing quietly at Moxie's side. 'This is Kuyhen,' Moxie said. 'She's been a prisoner in the old mine, taking care of weed plants for a bloke called Sunny Spells.'

Marianne and Judy had a way of looking at each other that let you know that they were actually telepathic. They did that look now. But they didn't say anything. Nobody seemed to know what to say, except for Non.

'I think you could do with some dinner!' she said to the child, and mimed eating. Kuhyen smiled again and let herself be led into the kitchen.

There was another awkward silence. Steph looked at the carpet, Judy reached for her knitting and Marianne for the remote. Moxie could hardly believe it!

'What?' she said. 'You aren't going to ask what's going on?'

Moxie stood in front of the telly and crossed her arms over her chest. 'This Sunny Spells bloke turned up tonight at ours with two of his helpers and threatened to burn the house down with us inside it.'

Another look passed between the Mams; that was a name they knew alright.

'I followed him and his men up to the mine,' Moxie went on. 'He's running a weed factory there and he was using Kuhyen as slave labour. I got her out. But he's got more kids coming. He wants to make the whole town into a factory for drugs.' Judy put her knitting down. Marianne, reached for Judy's hand.

'Spells said he'd *take* Ryan to make sure Dyl worked for him.'

Steph was sitting forward in her chair looking from Moxie to the Mams. 'Spells!' she said.

'Spells!' She looked daggers at her sister. *Didn't I tell you already*, her eyes seemed to say.

'There's history here,' Moxie declared. 'And I want to know what it is!'

To Moxie's surprise, Steph turned to Marianne and said another useful word, 'Tell.'

The Mams nodded.

The story came out haltingly at first as Judy and Marianne passed it back and forth between them, but by the time Non came back with Kuhyen and settled her under the blanket next to Ryan and the digger, it was beginning to flow more easily, 'Maybe they'll say which one is my actual Mam!' Non breathed into Moxie's ear.

They didn't of course but they *did* say that Dyl – Dylan Rees – *was* Ryan and Moxie's dad. He was from a village just a few miles away over the hills. An easy bus ride, back in the day when there had been buses.

'He was close to Steph and... all of us, really. A nice, quiet boy, at first.'

He can't have stayed quiet. He'd gone to prison six months before Moxie was born and came out a fully fledged hard man with a reputation that put him back inside soon after Ryan was born.

'Dyl and Steph never lived together,' Judy said. 'They weren't, like, *married* or anything.'

There were things the Mams were leaving out, Moxie could tell, but it would be no good asking. She just had to let them tell it their own way.

'Sunny Spells was a big noise in the valley towns when Dyl and Steph were growing up,' Marianne went on.

'Splashing the cash to make himself look good,' Judy added, 'Always on about "opportunities for our young people".'

Spells had funded youth clubs, including the one Dyl and Steph had gone to, but the only opportunities that Spells was really interested in were for himself. He recruited kids to work for him dealing drugs, and other jobs.

'The pretty ones, boys and girls, had it worst,' Marianne said. 'He had a lot of customers who liked pretty kids.'

Dyl and Steph must have been two of the prettiest. No wonder they had seemed so small and squashed in the presence of Sunny Spells, their old tyrant and tormentor.

'His downfall was the riding club. Your Gran, our Mam, Rhiannon Bowen, was a horsewoman,' Marianne told her. 'She got Spells to stump up for a kid's pony club here in the town.'

That was a lot to process! A gran? Moxie had never known she'd had one of those. And a gran who was a horsewoman! That had to be connected with the carvings on the stones.

'The ponies lived in the fields by the cemetery,' Marianne said, 'the ones that got chopped up when they built the bypass.'

That was where Piebald was now. Had she been one of Rhiannon's ponies all those years ago?

The Mams went on to tell how Spells had given Rhiannon money to build a riding school. Kids had come from all around, often given lifts to the club by Spells' friends in their big, posh cars. But rumours started about Spells and his mates and what they were *really* up to.

'Rhiannon wouldn't have it,' Marianne said. 'She defended him. Fell out with Steph big time. *Steph* knew first-hand what Spells was and how he harmed those kids.'

Moxie looked at Steph. There were tears rolling down her cheeks.

But it had been Rhiannon who found him out in the end. She caught him coming from the stables with a child he'd drugged.

'He claimed the kid was exhausted after riding and that he was taking him home,' Judy told Moxie, 'but Rhiannon had been a nurse. She knew a drugged child when she saw one.'

Rhiannon had confronted Spells, and it got

nasty. She was knocked out cold, and when she woke she was in the stables with the whole lot going up in flames around her. Rhiannon had only just got out.

'Spells got away, of course, the slimy bastard,' Judy added. 'He went abroad, we heard, and when they closed the UK borders after the last pandemic, well, we thought that's that. He can't come back.'

Where was Rhiannon now? Moxie wanted to ask, but a wild hammering on the front door silenced them all.

'Spells!' Steph said, and they all knew she was right.

'We'll hold them round the front for as long as we can,' Judy said.

'Go out the back,' Marianne added. 'Go and find Rhiannon. Tell her *he's back,* and this time we have to stop him.'

'How will I find her?' Moxie asked

'Follow your horse,' was all Marianne had time to say. 'Now get out of here!'

Keep off the roads and follow your horse. That wasn't much to go on, Moxie thought. She felt she should probably be very scared, yet something deep inside her was lit up like a flame.

9. Can't Say Goodbye

Non bundled Moxie, Ryan and Kuhyen out of the back door. The two children were groggily sleepy but thankfully didn't have to be carried. The shouting and banging coming from the street side of the house died down quite quickly and they both heard the sound of Spells' car growling back up the high street. Where was he going? They couldn't be sure. They still had to get away. They scuttled through the dark, more or less dragging the sleepy kids down muddy back alleys to the garage where Non kept the Wagon. Once inside, it felt a little safer.

Non lit a candle. It gave just enough light to make out the drifts of junk stored on the garage shelves. Moxie had teased Non many times about her hoarding, but she was glad of it now. Directed by Non, Moxie found sleeping bags and blankets, tin mugs and a saucepan. She shoved them in a backpack among the dust and cobwebs.

'I've never even been camping!' Moxie said.

'Is this mad, Non? Taking two kids to follow a horse god knows where?'

'Yeah, it is quite mad,' Non replied. 'But it can't be far to Rhiannon's place, if the horse really did walk here, can it?'

Moxie shrugged. How far could horses walk? She had no idea.

'Anyway, Mox,' Non went on, 'this Spells is the worst kind of bad news. Bottom line, you just have to get these kids away from him.'

Moxie nodded. That *was* the bottom line.

Unless Dyl had blabbed, Spells didn't even know Moxie existed, so she could skirt around town and get to Piebald in reasonable safety, but he would be looking for Ryan, and although he might not know yet that Kuhyen had escaped, he'd know if he saw her. So Non would take them up to the cemetery hidden on the floor of the Wagon. Moxie shouldered the pack and got ready to leave. She put her arm round Ryan.

'You and Kuhyen are gonna play a game with Non,' Moxie told him. 'You're gonna hide in the Wagon until you get to Piebald, and then we're going on an adventure.'

Ryan grinned. 'Bring digger?' he asked.

Moxie nodded. 'Yeah, I think Digger should definitely come with us.'

Dark was seeping out of the eastern sky by

the time Moxie slipped the halter over Piebald's head and led her through the gate. Non brought two old supermarket bags out of the Wagon, the kind with long handles. Tied over Piebald's back, they were like saddle bags. Somehow, Non had got hold of a box of Coco Pops, some packets of crackers, matches and a big plastic bottle of water. These went into the 'saddle bags' along with Ryan's digger.

'You are amazing, Non!' Moxie said.

Moxie lifted the kids onto Piebald's back, Ryan, who was the biggest, behind and little Kuhyen in front. Ryan was floppy with sleepiness, but Kuhyen's eyes shone and she showed at once that she was very used to horses. She took Ryan's arms and put them round her waist to stop him slipping off and took a handful of mane between her fingers. Moxie gave her a thumbs up sign, which she returned, along with a smile.

Non drove the Wagon beside them as far as the cemetery gates. It was getting light now and it would be best if they were gone before people were awake to see and to tell tales. Moxie leant down to the Wagon's door.

'What do you think Marianne meant when she said, "This time we're gonna stop him?"' Moxie asked. Non shook her head.

'I dunno, but maybe when I go back now I'll find out.'

Moxie nodded. 'I'm leaving you with another Mam to look out for. I'm sorry, Non.'

'That's all right, Mox. Give her a jigsaw and she's no trouble.'

Non was smiling, but Mox could see it was a stuck-on smile, not a real one.

'I can't say goodbye, can you?' Non said. 'It's weird, isn't it?'

'Yeah,' Moxie agreed. 'Really weird. Let's not do it then.'

'OK, we won't. Just take this instead of goodbye.'

Non pulled something from her pocket and put it into Moxie's hand.

'A mobile phone?' Moxie said. 'When did this last work? Is it a lucky charm, Non?'

Non frowned. 'Maybe,' she said. 'Maybe not. I'm working on something. Just take it, OK?'

Non closed the Wagon door and drove off. Moxie watched the funny little car vanish into the underpass. Neither of them waved. Moxie shoved the little phone into the zip pocket of her tracksuit. Non was as weird as her two mams sometimes.

The sun was coming up. The town was behind them now, and in front of them the two sides of the valley rose up, clothed in trees and bushes and ringing with birdsong in the late spring dawn. Moxie had never heard birds being so loud before. She looked up at the children, Ryan with his chin over Kuhyen's shoulder as if he'd known her all his life, and Kuhyen only just awake enough to stop them falling off but still more alive than she'd seemed a few hours ago.

Moxie scratched behind Piebald's ears. The horse gave a soft whiny. 'OK then, Piebald. Which way? Which way to Rhiannon?' Piebald pushed her nose into Moxie's neck, tossed her head so the reins hung looser, then pricked up her ears and began to move.

Moxie expected her to head straight up the side of the valley to the right of the cemetery, where a path led away from the last few houses straggled at the edge of the town. But she didn't. Instead, she followed the outer wall of the cemetery, over the rough grass where it parted from the line of the road, then down the hill, instead of up, and through an overgrown field littered with rusting farm equipment and the usual supply of abandoned cars. They came to a stand of dark conifers with the remains of many bonfires, charred bits of furniture, broken bottles, plastic melted into lumps, then along a well-worn track that looped back from the end of the copse towards town. Moxie had been here lots of times. So had every other kid in town. It was where you came for your first fag, your first spliff, your first snog.

'Where are we going?' The horse stopped, reached down and absently grabbed and ate a mouthful of grass. She looked at Moxie with her piebald eyes, that seemed, right now, as lacking in intelligence as marbles. This was crazy, Moxie thought. They were relying on a horse for guidance? She tightened her grip on the bridle.

'C'mon, girl,' Moxie said gently. 'I think we need to go back the other way.'

But the horse pulled from Moxie's grasp and walked on. She pushed through a screen of bushes and in amongst the trees. There, behind low-hanging branches, was a narrow path that Moxie had never seen before. Piebald knew exactly where she was going.

10. Playtime

They went on through the rows of dark trees then out the other side onto a slope covered with tussocks of grass, no roads in sight. Even though Moxie had looked up at the hills above the town all her life, she hadn't really understood that there was so much space with no roads in it. Although they hadn't come far, the town was already hidden behind a fold of hill. As far as anyone in town was concerned, they had vanished. Had Piebald known this? Moxie couldn't be sure, but knowing that they were safe from prying eyes did make her relax a little.

The path climbed quite steeply, up the sloping brow of one hill and then down into the fold between two more. They passed between more ruined buildings and sheer rockfaces like bites out of the hill, where stone had been quarried. The ground beside the path here looked as if someone had mowed it, but the bobbing white tails of rabbits showed who was really responsible.

'Bunny!' Ryan exclaimed, suddenly wide awake and bolt upright on Piebald's back.

'*Contho!*' Kuhyen said quietly, and pointed at another little brown bum disappearing down a burrow.

Moxie pointed too. '*Contho?*' she asked, and Kuhyen smiled and repeated the word. Whatever language Kuhyen spoke, Moxie was pleased that she'd just learned her first word in it.

Kuhyen rubbed her tummy with the hand that wasn't deep in Piebald's mane, then pointed to her mouth. '*Do an?*' she said. Moxie nodded. She didn't need a translation to understand.

'Yeah, you're right, we need food, and a sleep.'

They sat together on a big flat stone against a wall as the sun rose and warmed them. They were all so tired and hungry that even dry cereal washed down with cold water felt good. Moxie got out a blanket to cover Kuhyen and Ryan, who accepted one another like a couple of puppies and fell asleep at once. She told herself that she should stay awake and keep watch, but she had been awake now for more than twenty-four hours and keeping her eyes open was impossible. If Piebald could navigate, then Moxie guessed she could also stand guard.

The sun was much higher when Moxie woke. By the looks of things, not a great deal of guarding had been going on. Piebald was flat out on the grass, her eyes closed, gently farting in the sunshine. Moxie sat up and listened. There wasn't a single human sound anywhere apart from Ryan's little snores; both he and Kuhyen were fast asleep still. Good. Moxie needed some peace and privacy for a few minutes. She wasn't used to doing without a toilet and she didn't want to be hurried over her first outside 'go'. She grabbed a bit of loo roll from the supermarket saddle bag and set off to find a bush.

It wasn't as bad as she expected – in fact, it was quite nice, squatting in the open air with the sun on her back. But just as she had finished, she heard screaming. She pulled up her pants and ran, convinced that somehow they had been followed and found. But it wasn't that kind of screaming. It was the screaming of two children and a horse chasing each other round a big rock in an improvised mixture of tag and hide and seek. Moxie stood back and watched them. The kids were crouching on one side of the rock, barely suppressing their giggles, shushing each other. Piebald was creeping round the other side, her head low, her ears forward; if a horse could be said to tiptoe, then Piebald was tiptoeing. She crept the other way around behind the children and breathed on them. They both screeched, leapt up and ran, and Piebald kicked up her heels and ran after them.

When in her life had Moxie ever been able to *play* like that? Not at school; the brief time she was there was before her operation. School had been a trial of taunts and teasing that she had been glad to quit. After that, she had Ryan to care for, and soon after *that*, Ryan *and* Mam. She'd never been chased screaming in the sunshine. Moxie found her eyes prickling with tears. No! *No*, she would *not* cry. She didn't do crying. She pulled the threatening tears back inside and called out, 'Stop making such a noise! Eat some more. We might have a long old way to go!'

They left the old quarry behind and climbed down into a small, scrub-filled valley, then up and over the shoulder of another hill, then another, and another. The slopes were clothed in white-barked trees with curtains of bright green leaves, shushing and shivering in the breeze. Little streams tumbled around rocks and small birds called. It was like a fairy story. Moxie couldn't believe that all this had been here all the days of her life, just a few hours' walk out of the town.

There was no path now, so they were relying on Piebald to know the way, but the further they went, the surer the horse seemed to be about their direction. There was no sign of Piebald's usual 'shamble a bit, graze a bit' style; she was on a mission, and Moxie struggled to keep up. She wasn't used to walking up and down hills with a pack on her back. It took all her concentration to keep going, so it was a very good thing that although Kuhyen could scream and giggle like a little kid, once on Piebald's back she was very grown up. She knew just what to do to keep herself and Ryan safe as they rode, pulling Ryan to lean forward over Piebald's neck as they climbed and making him lean back when they descended. What was more, she kept Ryan amused by trading words, finding each other's pronunciation hysterically funny.

'Leaf,' Ryan would point and say.

'*Lacay*,' Kuhyen replied.

'Horse.'

'*Ngua*.'

Given how Ryan struggled with his own language, it was amazing to Moxie that he was so keen to learn an entirely unfamiliar one. Moxie found herself looking at the slight little girl and wondering more and more what her story was.

On and on they went, hour after hour. By the time the sun began to slide toward the hilltops, Moxie's legs ached, Kuhyen had fallen silent and Ryan kept asking over and over, 'Where are we going, Moxie?'

Moxie's answer, 'To find Gran', made no sense to Ry, because that wasn't really a destination, and anyway, he'd never heard of having a gran. But Ry being Ry, he kept asking, ever-optimistic of a more satisfying reply.

At the top of one particularly difficult slope, Piebald paused, her sides heaving. 'Off you get, you two,' Moxie told the children. 'She needs a rest, and you need to stretch your legs.' (And shut up asking me the same thing, Ry, Moxie thought.)

They slid off Piebald's back and Kuhyen once again took charge of Ryan, heading off his threatened whining by grabbing his hand and bouncing off up the slope ahead. Moxie slipped the pack from her shoulders and slid down; never mind Piebald needing a rest, she was knackered. But Piebald didn't want to rest. She grew agitated. She whinnied and stamped her feet, then set off again, without Moxie. There was no choice but to shoulder the pack and hurry after the horse and the children.

Without a load to carry, Piebald picked up her pace. Up and up she went, zig-zagging around rocks and between trees. Moxie thought her legs would explode, and even Kuhyen seemed to have run out of bounce. Just at the point when nothing was going to stop Ryan from losing his positivity and having a meltdown about walking uphill *forever*, they came out onto a wide hilltop. While they'd been under the tree cover they hadn't seen the clouds gathering all around. They were dark and purple as a bruise and already grumbling with thunder. There was going to be a storm, one of those big ones that had gotten more frequent. Without the trees, they'd have no shelter at all. Moxie called to Piebald and the children, who were now quite far ahead. Then she noticed it: a little stone barn nestled in a knot of bushes. That's where Piebald was headed; she knew there was going to be a storm and she'd brought them to a shelter, just in time.

11. Big Weather

The three humans and the piebald horse watched the rain come down and the darkness fall. Fat veins of lightning cracked the sky open and lit everything in blinks of neon brightness. Moxie reckoned that big storms were the silver lining of what people called the climate emergency. She loved the crash and flash of it all and Ry had learned from her to love it too. But seeing a storm from inside a house was rather different from watching it from the inside of a leaky three-walled barn. It wasn't much of a shelter, and the rain blew in. Piebald stood just inside the entrance, which helped to keep the wet at bay, but all the same, Moxie and the children had to huddle by the back wall to keep dry.

Kuhyen was blankly stoical, but Ryan's positivity was failing him. 'I want to go home!' he said. 'Go home *now*.'

'Come on, Ry,' Moxie said. 'It'll be fun. We'll light a fire.'

Immediately, Ryan perked up, but how, Moxie wondered, would she make a fire without wood? She had never lit a fire outdoors in her life, but she could at least manage light. She reached into the pack and pulled out the torch that Non had given her. It was a bit rubbish, but better than sitting in the dark.

'This is a proper adventure, eh, Ry?' she said, and Ryan, bless him, beamed and allowed her to feed him crackers and wrap him in a blanket.

'Adventure!' he said with his mouth full.

It had felt like an adventure, climbing up the hills in the sunlight, discovering this whole new world, but in the middle of a storm and pouring rain it just felt miserable, and a bit stupid, to be following a *horse* to find a person they'd never met in a place they didn't have an address for. There was only enough cereal for one more breakfast and the crackers were nearly all gone. If they didn't find this Rhiannon tomorrow, they were going to be hungry. And then what? Walk home to find Spells waiting for them all?

Moxie posted another cracker into Ryan's mouth. 'Where's Kuhyen?' he asked, his mouth still full.

Moxie's heart turned over. Where *was* Kuhyen? She'd been here a moment ago, and now she'd vanished. Was there something horrible lurking in the storm outside or in the dark of the barn? Just as Moxie's mind imagined a horror story, the girl stepped back into the circle of weak torchlight with handfuls of sheep wool and dried sheep poo.

'Fire!' she said, then mimed the striking of a match. Moxie dug in their baggage once more, pulled out a box of matches and handed them over. Kuhyen made a little mound of wool and dried poo and shielded it with her body. She struck a match and the flame leaped into the dry wool and grew. Gently, Kuhyen blew on it. To Moxie's astonishment, it began to burn! They had a fire! It was small, smokey and smelly, but the storm felt less scary and the night less dark.

They found more poo and some bits of wood too. The fire crackled and spat, but it did give out a bit of heat. Moxie made a hot mush of coco pops and fed Ryan and Kuhyen like birds, which set the two of them giggling again. Piebald lay down just inside the door with her legs folded under her like a cat. When Ryan fell asleep, Moxie laid a sleeping bag on the floor and put him in it as far as she could manage. Then she draped a blanket around Kuhyen's shoulders.

'Thank!' said Kuyhen.

Moxie sat back down beside the girl. 'You are very good at riding.' Moxie gestured to Piebald.

'Good with horses.'

'Many horse at home,' Kuhyen replied.

'Where is your home?'

Kuyhen shook her head and waved a hand in the air. 'Far. Far,' she said. 'Boat many, many days.' The girl hugged her knees and rested her face on them. When she looked up again, Moxie could see she had been crying. 'Bad man. Bad Spells. Steal many child.'

Moxie thought of what Marianne had said, *this time we have to stop him*. Yes, Spells had to be stopped, but right now Moxie couldn't see how.

Kuhyen fell asleep and Moxie put her into a sleeping bag. The storm crashed on, Moxie's tummy rumbled and the poo-fire stank. Her brain whirred around, going over and over all that had happened. She would *never* get to sleep.

She realised she *had* fallen asleep when she woke up with a dead arm and sheep poo in her hair. The two kids were spark out and Piebald was no longer filling the doorway. She must be outside. Moxie got up and tottered through the open side of the barn. The storm had passed, but had left behind a chilly fog, thick as smoke. She couldn't see anything, but Piebald wouldn't be far away, surely?

'Piebald!' Moxie called. 'Piebald!'

The mist swallowed her voice as if her mouth

had been covered with a cushion. She called again and listened for Piebald's answering whinny. But there was nothing. Moxie walked a little further from the barn and called again. The mist felt too empty; too silent. Where was Piebald? Moxie's heart raced and the bottom of her stomach sort of dropped out. What had happened? Had Piebald gone out and been struck by lightning? Had she just wandered off because she'd never really been leading them anywhere and was just a pony with no more brain than a chicken? Moxie walked further and called until her voice turned croaky. She was panicking. She *must* calm down. Piebald had probably just been getting some grassy breakfast and was now back in the barn.

But when Moxie spun round to head back to the barn, it had gone. There was nothing to see but white mist. She walked a few paces and found she was in a bog, suddenly up to her knees in water. She hadn't walked through water on the way here, had she? She called out to Ryan and somewhere, quite far off and to her left, she thought she heard his voice. Well, *a* voice anyway. She ran that way, stumbling over the soggy ground.

'Ry? Ry?'

Now there were voices coming from the other

direction. But surely that wasn't Ryan? Had Spells tracked them to the barn? Moxie's feet found solid ground and she ran as hard as she could towards the sound of what she thought were voices. The fog swirled around her and the sound of her heart drowned out everything else.

She tried to think, tried to work out which way she should go, but all that filled her head was a jumble of nightmares: Spells snapping his fingers under Mam's nose, Dyl being punched by the thugs, a woman running from a burning stable, fists hammering on the Mams' front door. It was like thunder in her head, a pounding that grew closer, that surrounded her, and in which she feared she'd drown.

It wasn't thunder. It was hooves – the running feet of piebald horses pounding on the ground. They came out of the white curtain of fog like a magic trick and ploughed up the soft earth as they stopped suddenly in front of Moxie. They tossed their wild manes, stamping and huffing warm breath into the dawn cold. One pushed to the front and came towards her.

'Piebald!' As Moxie threw her arms around the pony's neck, one last horse arrived, a horse with a woman on its back who spoke her name in a soft rasp. 'Moxie Bowen! Moxie Bowen!'

12. Gran's House

Rhiannon was pleased to see Moxie and Ryan, that was clear. Kuhyen too seemed welcome. But there had been no hugs, no torrent of questions. The old woman seemed shy, almost afraid to meet a human glance. Moxie concluded that she had simply lived up here alone with her horses for far too long and was probably as addicted as her daughter Marianne to 'not telling you things'.

It was quite a distance to Rhiannon's house from the barn. Piebald carried Ryan and Kuhyen and Rhiannon gave Moxie a horse called Pendy; another horse took the saddlebags and back pack. The rest of the herd flowed around them and they moved together like one creature through the blankness of the fog. It was like one of those dreams where you run and run and get nowhere at all.

Moxie looked sideways at Rhiannon. She was very old, her skin brown and crinkled with the outdoors. Her hair grew in dark messy tufts that had clearly been cut off as soon as they got long enough to require attention. Small and skinny, she moved like a young woman, almost with the quickness of a child.

At last, as the sun rose, a breeze began to tug at the fog, revealing a sea of hills that stretched unbroken from horizon to horizon. All the human things were tucked down out of sight, in the valleys. The only house visible was a low, dark smudge in the distance that Moxie assumed must be Rhiannon's home.

With the mist, and the quiet it held, gone, Moxie felt it was time to get her grandmother to speak. She'd had enough of that odd, shy silence. 'How did you find us?' she asked. Easy questions first, Moxie thought. Rhiannon still didn't look at her, but at least she answered promptly and didn't seem put out.

'Melys came in the storm. She got me out of bed!'

'Who is Melys?'

Rhiannon pointed at Piebald. 'Your friend,' she said.

'Oh, *Piebald*,' Moxie said. 'She just turned up one day, dirty and half-starved. So we took care of her.'

Rhiannon's look softened. 'She just went off one day,' the old woman said. 'I didn't see her go. She just decided for herself.' She shook her head and looked away. 'I might have guessed where she'd gone, I suppose.'

What did *that* mean? Moxie was thoroughly irritated now.

'*You might have guessed where she'd gone,*' Moxie cried. 'You meet your grandchildren after who knows how many years and that's all you can say?'

Moxie didn't wait for an answer. She kicked Pendy's sides and urged him to trot. It looked like a straight run to the low house on the horizon and she'd bet the horse knew the fastest way to his stables. Maybe there would even be a proper toilet; she was pretty sick of all the kinds of shit she'd had to deal with recently. Pendy didn't seem to mind leaving his mistress and his mates behind. He struck out at a good pace and Moxie urged him on, her body remembering – to her surprise – how to synchronise with a fast-moving horse. Soon they were flying over the grass, and there was nothing at all in Moxie's head but the light, the sky and the rhythm of Pendy's hooves.

There was an outside loo in a little hut between the barn and the very nice stables, where Pendy went to find some breakfast. A verandah ran all along the front of the little house. Moxie sat in the rocking chair there and watched the horses and the riders grow slowly larger. As they drew closer, the horses began to disperse, scattering to graze. Rhiannon dismounted, took the bridle from her mount and the 'pack' horse and said a word into their ears. The horses ran off to join their friends, like children at playtime. Rhiannon helped Ryan and Kuhyen down from Piebald's back and removed the bridle, but Piebald didn't run off. Instead, she walked beside the humans as they came up to the house.

Rhiannon looked more like a proper granny now. She held both the children's hands and was listening and smiling as Ryan spoke. She stopped at the bottom of the steps up to the verandah and looked at Moxie properly for the first time.

'I'm sorry,' she began. 'We will have a proper good talk. Let's get these two little ones fed first though, eh?' Rhiannon smiled then, a smile somehow so familiar and so sad that it made Moxie's eyes prickle again. *That's twice in as many days. You are getting proper soft, Moxie Bowen*, Moxie scolded herself, but she smiled back and nodded.

A bit later, Rhiannon dragged another rocker out onto the verandah and she and Moxie sat with their hands round their mugs, watching the children throwing straw at each other.

'I had forgotten how much children will eat when they are really hungry,' Rhiannon said.

Moxie didn't comment. It felt lovely to be here. It would have felt even lovelier to have been here more often. To have had a gran in her life all these long years, taking care of Mam and Ryan.

'I've got a lot of questions,' Moxie blurted. 'Like, where the hell have you been all this time? But how about you start by just telling me, I dunno... *everything*!'

Rhiannon looked at Moxie over the top of her mug. 'Still a force of nature then, Moxie,' she said. 'OK. But it might be as hard for you to hear as it is for me to tell.'

13. Mam

Rhiannon began by shaking her head. 'I may not be the grandmother that you were hoping for, Moxie,' she said, 'and I may not be the grandmother that you want.'

'I think you are the granny I remember,' Moxie replied. 'When Piebald, I mean Melys, came, I remembered someone who put me on the back of a horse and told me I was a natural. That must have been you.'

Rhiannon nodded sadly. 'You were. You still are. You've a way with horses that you were born with. Melys saw it in you from the start. I brought her down to town to visit you when she was just a colt really. You took to each other. But we had to stop coming because Steph was too angry with me. She didn't want me to have anything to do with you.'

'Why was my mum angry with you?' Moxie asked.

'Is she still angry?' Rhiannon replied.

'Hard to tell *what* she is these days. Her brain

is fried. It has been since Ryan was a toddler. I take care of both of them.'

'I didn't know,' Rhiannon said quietly. 'I'm sorry.'

Sorry for what? Moxie thought. That you didn't know? That you didn't ask? Moxie took a breath. Being angry with her Gran wasn't going to get them anywhere.

'Don't you go to school?' Rhiannon said.

'No one goes to school in our town now,' Moxie snapped. 'The nearest school is twenty miles away. That doesn't matter, Gran. Start at the beginning.'

Rhiannon shook her head. 'The beginning is too long ago, Moxie. I'll start at the end. The end you know. The fire.'

'The night you found out what Spells was really up to?'

Rhiannon nodded and laced her fingers more tightly round her mug. 'Yes. Though looking back I can't imagine how I didn't see it. Perhaps I didn't *want* to see.'

Her face clouded like last night's sky, full of bad memories and guilt. It couldn't be much fun being Rhiannon, Moxie thought. 'Is that why Mam was angry with you?' she asked. 'Marianne said you'd fallen out over it.'

Rhiannon nodded again. 'I didn't see Spells for

what he was. I didn't protect Steph. No wonder she was angry. But it's more what happened with the fire.' Rhiannon stopped looking at Moxie now. This was the part she really didn't want to tell. But Moxie wasn't going to let her stop.

'Go on,' she said. '*Go on*!'

Rhiannon closed her eyes. 'Everybody must have seen the smoke. I think half of Cemetery Street pulled me out. They all kept asking *if there was anyone else inside*. I said the kid, Matty – Matty Thomas. The one Spells had drugged. We found him, they said. Is there someone else?' Gran's voice filled with the panic it must have had on that night. She went on, her words coming like gasps between breaths of smoke. 'I said no, because I thought she was with Steph. But she was in the stables. Drugged like Matty. Maybe she caught Spells with the boy... I don't know. Then Steph came and said, "Where is she?" And then I knew. We sent them in to look, but it was too late. She died in hospital. They only saved *you*.'

'What are you talking about, Gran – *saving me*? This was before I was born... wasn't it? Who died?

Moxie's heart stood still. Before the answer came, she'd guessed it.

'My *other* daughter,' Rhiannon put her face into her hands. 'Florence Bowen. She was pregnant with Dylan's baby.'

It was too much to take in, and for a few minutes Moxie thought she couldn't even breathe. She needed space. Gran understood. She said she'd watch Ryan and Kuhyen and feed them yet more toast and blackberry jam. Dear Piebald – Moxie would struggle to get used to calling the horse Melys – carried her out and out and out onto the wide hills, until everything was in the distance, small enough to see but not to hurt.

Moxie lay looking up at the sky, her head resting on Piebald's neck. It was all a mess, but none of it was surprising when you thought about it. Of course Steph was angry over Florence, so she'd taken Moxie from her grandmother and tried to raise her herself. But Steph was only seventeen and already too damaged by what Spells and his crew had got her into to take care of anyone, even herself. No surprise that when Dyl got out of prison they ended up trying to comfort each other in some crazy way and ended up with Ryan. And no surprise that Steph couldn't cope with her own baby any more than she had with her sister's, so she'd fried her brain with drugs and alcohol.

And through it all Rhiannon's guilt had kept her on a mountaintop with a bunch of horses. No one had ever, ever, ever told Moxie about her own mother because it had all been just too painful for them to think about!

Moxie was furious with all of them. She screamed at the sky, but Piebald took no notice and just lay still, and after a while Moxie lay still too. She leant back against Piebald's big, comforting body; she felt the solid earth beneath her. She took a long, long breath. Angry didn't help. Angry just felt like rocks in your heart. She would let it go, sink down into the ground and go back to the fiery heart of the planet where it could do no harm.

The horses cast long, leggy shadows as Moxie arrived back at the house. Rhiannon had given Ryan and Kuhyen a pot of black paint and a brush each. She was letting them paint whatever they wanted on the wall of the verandah. Moxie walked up the steps and smiled at Rhiannon.

'What other gran would let kids graffiti her house!' Rhiannon said, then looked away. 'I'm not much good with kids,' she said.

'Huh!' Moxie said. 'I think that's obviously crap!' Moxie sat in the other rocker. 'I've been thinking,' she said. 'You blame yourself for Florence. I blame Steph for being a rubbish parent. I blame Dyl and you for not being there. But the real person to blame is Spells.'

Rhiannon nodded. She took Moxie's hand and squeezed it. It was too much to look at each other, so they looked at the shapes spidering over the wall. Ryan's were a joyful jumble that he probably understood but no one else would, but Kuhyen's picture was clear as day. A house by a river, a lot of children, horses and animals; a child being held by the arm; a boatload of small kids with big black tears falling into the waves. What Spells had done to Moxie's family was pretty mild compared with what he was doing to families like Kuhyen's.

'He's coming back to the mine on Wednesday night with a load more kids like her,' Moxie said. 'He wants to make the whole town into his drugs factory. We have to stop him, Gran.'

Rhiannon hung her head and sighed. 'I should have stopped him years ago. Why didn't I see what he was? Why didn't I do something then?' Her voice was dripping with guilt. Moxie couldn't stand it.

'Stop it!' she said. 'Just bloody stop beating yourself up. It's pointless. It doesn't help. We can do something *now*, can't we? Can't we, Gran?'

Slowly, as if she was pulling her whole self up from the bottom of a pit, Rhiannon sat up, sat taller. She looked at Moxie, and Moxie felt she was seeing this woman for the very first time. Her eyes were no longer muddy brown but flecked with green flame. When she spoke, her voice was strong and straight as a sword. 'We can, my girl, we can,' she said. 'Because we are the *Marchogion Rhydd,* the ancient free horsewomen of these hills, me and you too, and it's high time and more that we rode again.'

14. High We Live and Free

'You are heiress to a long tradition,' Rhiannon told Moxie. 'There have been Marchogion Rhydd since humans first came to these hills. Women chosen by the blood in their veins to ride for vengeance and for justice.'

These women, Rhiannon explained, lived ordinary lives day to day, but when they were needed they gathered on the open hills. In life, no one might know who they were, but their graves were always marked with a piebald horse.

'Once,' Rhiannon said, 'the horsewomen passed messages by speaking to the birds, so horses and women were called to arms by ravens and swallows.'

'But we have moved with the times,' she added as she climbed a ladder onto the roof of the house and balanced up there between the solar panels. The megaphone hanging around her neck by its strap crackled as she turned it on, but then her voice boomed out:

'Esgyn yn uchel, byw yn rhydd
rhwng y nen a'n meirch,
ymhell o rwymau dyletswyddau,
neb yn gaeth i ddyn, na dynes chwaith.
Dawn ac ysbryd yn ein gwaed
yn trosglwyddo o fam i ferch.
Carlamu tua'r golau
a gwynebu'r tywyllwch.
Fel ein ceffylau,
ni yw'r sêr llachar
a düwch angau.
Gwyliwch ni nawr, rydym yn eich plith!'

'High we live and free
between sky and our horses' backs
beyond the shackles of duty,
no man's slave nor no woman's either.
Our skill and spirit passed in blood,
mother onto daughter.
We ride for the light.
We wield the darkness.
Like our horses we are
the white of starlight
and black of death.
Watch now, we are among you!'

In Welsh, which Moxie didn't speak, the words seemed like some kind of spell, or maybe just a way of calling horses in for dinner. Spell or menu, it did the trick. Within an hour, a huge herd of black and white horses more than two hundred strong was milling round the house. Moxie helped Rhiannon drag sacks of pony nuts, bales of hay and buckets of water into the yard to feed and water them. Ryan and Kuhyen watched from the verandah, delighted and amazed, exclaiming to each other in a mixture of languages.

When the horses had finished eating, Rhiannon said it was time to go. She handed Moxie a steak knife and a head torch.

'What are these for?' Moxie said.

'We used to carry swords and flaming brands, but like I said, we have to move with the times,' Rhiannon answered.

'What are we going to actually *do*, Gran?'

Rhiannon smiled. 'We are going to scare the living shit out of that bastard Spells. When he delivers the kids to the mine, we'll be waiting.'

'What, you, me and all these horses?'

'And the horsewomen. You'll see. C'mon, we have to ride.'

'Can I ride Melys?' Moxie asked.

'I don't think Melys would carry anyone else into battle. We'll put the kids on Pandy and leave them somewhere safe.'

Into battle? Moxie thought. *Really*? Really!

It was a gorgeous day. Moisture rose from the grass in shining strands. They took a different route from the one Melys had led them on. It went over the spines of the hills and skirted the edge of lakes to bring them round the other side of town, into the wooded slope above the mine. By dusk, the herd was scattered between the trees waiting, their piebald patterns breaking up their outline in the shadows, so they all but disappeared.

Moxie left Kuhyen and Ryan eating more jam sandwiches and went to speak to Rhiannon. 'What's the plan, then?'

'I need to get a message to Marianne,' Rhiannon said, 'so she can call the Marchogion. I can't use the megaphone. It might let Spells know we're here!'

Moxie smiled. 'Yeah, it might. I could go?'

Rhiannon shook her head. 'He might know about you now, Moxie, and you are distinctive.'

Moxie was about to suggest having a chat to a bird when a sound they hadn't heard in years came from Moxie's pocket. The phone! Non's mobile phone had got a *message*! Moxie and Rhiannon stared at each other in amazement.

'Well get it out and see what it says!' Rhiannon commanded.

It was a simple phone, the oldest kind, not one that did anything clever, like take pictures of your bum, for instance, or show you cats drinking out of cocktail glasses. It just did phone things: texts and talking.

'*Text me when you get this, Non,*' it said. Moxie's thumbs had almost forgotten what to do, but they soon remembered.

Moxie: *How d'you get this to work?*

Non: *I'm an unrecognised genius. It'll only do text tho. Where are you? It's mad here. Spells' thugs all over the place. It's like an invasion. Steph was freaking out so Marianne took her to Judy's gran's old house on Mount Street last night. Spells don't know about that house. Where are you?*

Moxie: *With Rhiannon. Rhiannon says tell Judy to put out the call. Tell them to come the back way to the woods behind the mine.*

Non: *WTF? What call? Who to?*

Moxie: *I dunno. Just do it, Non. Gran says Judy'll understand.*

Non: *OK, but what's going on?*

Moxie: *We're gonna put the frighteners on Spells. Where is Dyl?*

Non: *Haven't seen him since you left. Reckon he's done a runner. Where's Ry and the little kid?*

Moxie: *Here. I need to get them somewhere safe before things kick off.*

Non: *What things kick off?*

Moxie: *No time to explain, Non.*

Non: *OK. Get them to the trees at the end of the old football pitch. I'll bring the Wagon. Spells' lot don't think a one-legged woman is much of a threat. I can swing by Judy's Gran's and check on our Mams.*

Moxie: *OK, leaving now.*

It was easy to make the run between the trees a game for Ryan, but Kuhyen definitely understood things were more serious. As soon as they saw the Wagon trundling through the dusk over the old pitch, they made a dash for it. The kids got into the Wagon and it vanished into the shadows. At least the kids were safe. Moxie sighed with relief and ran back up to the mine. She'd be a racing snake if she had any more days like this.

By the time she got back, 'the call' had done its work. Ten riders had gathered in a dim clearing and were greeting each other quietly. Even in the poor light, Moxie knew the women well. They were familiar old ladies who gossiped outside the shop, made Welsh cakes for their grandkids and had their hair done on Fridays. But they looked nothing like their usual selves. Mounted on their piebald horses, with stout sticks held like swords, they seemed to glow in the darkness.

'We're here to get rid of Spells once and for all,' Rhiannon announced. 'He wants to rule this town and do his evil and we're going to stop him. I know it's been a while, but we need to be prepared.' She looked around the ring of faces in the failing light and gathered their nods.

'OK. Each of you take a herd of twenty. Moxie, you're with me. Stay hidden, wait as quietly as you can.'

They didn't have to wait long.

15. The Pony Club

The lights of three vehicles snaked down the track, two black SUVs and a van. They parked up in an arc so that their headlights lit up the big space in front of the metal doors. The two Sofas got out of the first car, then five identikit thugs from the second. They swaggered around for a minute, then gave the all-clear for Spells to get out of the car. He went to the metal doors, undid the padlocks and opened them up to reveal the bright green space inside. Two more men got out of the van, unlocked its back doors and dragged out eight children, smaller than Kuhyen, tied together by their wrists. They were wailing with fear. Piebald's body tensed, sensing Moxie's anger; next to them, Rhiannon breathed hard in the dark.

'We'll wait until they step away from the cars,' she said. 'Another minute.'

Spells was unlocking the metal grid, the inner gate, ready to put the children into their prison. Without Dyl, he was having to do his own dirty work. Where was Dyl? Moxie wondered. Had he just run off and abandoned them after bringing all this trouble to their door? Moxie pushed the thought aside. She *would not* think of that now.

'Now!' Rhiannon said. She raised her hand to pass the signal to the next rider and her gang of horses and urged Pandy forwards.

Moxie had imagined a gallop, but instead a line of riders and horses just melted out of the woods. They were so quiet, and the men so occupied, that by the time they noticed that anything was happening they were surrounded.

The Marchogion and about thirty of the horses bore down on the entrance. There was nowhere for the men to run except into the building. The ring steadily tightened, then Rhiannon held up a hand and they drew to a halt. Spells was doing his best to hide his discomfort. The men were openly afraid.

'So, it's the woman who torched her own daughter. Hello, Rhiannon.'

Moxie glanced at her Gran, but the Rhiannon who'd been crippled by her own guilt was nowhere to be seen. She ignored his words entirely.

'You have one chance, Spells,' she said. 'Hand over those children, take your men and leave and that will be the end of it.'

'Or what? You and your pony club here will do some very tricky dressage?' he sneered. 'Forgive me if I don't feel threatened by a bunch of old biddies and their nags. I own this town. I own your family. In fact, I've *got* your family. So I'll do what I like here.'

Moxie felt sick. What did he mean? Surely Non and Ryan and the rest were all safe, hidden from Spells in Judy's mum's house.

'You're bluffing, Spells,' Rhiannon said. 'Last chance now.'

'It's your funeral,' Spells smirked. 'Or rather, *theirs*.'

Rhiannon didn't flinch. She held up her hand again and the rest of the horses came out of the trees and began to move towards the men. They gained speed so fast it made Moxie gasp. A wave of hooves smashed every window of every car and pierced every tyre. Some of the men tried to break through the moving circle of horses, some tried to grab the riders. They were simply trampled and kicked aside. For a moment the two Sofas and Spells held their ground at the entrance to the factory, alongside the screaming line of children. Then they ran in between the plants, with one of the Sofas grasping the arm of the last child in the line. Tied together as they were, the children were hard to drag. They tripped and tangled and the man was forced to let go. He, Spells and the other Sofa vanished amongst the greenery.

They would not get away.

'Come on, Melys. Get after them.'

Melys wasn't an elegant horse, but she could turn a corner pretty fast. They raced in under the bright lights, down the avenues of tall green plants that seemed to go on for miles. She was gaining on them, when all the lights went out. In the sudden dark, she and Melys crashed into a knot of toppled plants whose branches snatched the head torch right off Moxie's face. Moxie went one way and the horse went another. It took a minute to recover, by which time a blast of cool night air told Moxie that the men had escaped through a side door. Moxie led Melys out through it to see the path the men had taken. There at the end of a track was the Wagon, on its side like a discarded toy.

I've got your family.

Yes, Moxie thought, you have, but not for long. On a wave of white hot anger, Moxie rode out through the metal gates.

'They're getting away down the hillside,' she yelled, and together the Marchogion wheeled around and thundered down the hill towards the road.

Whoever Spells had paid to work for him, they were nowhere now. He had no friends and just four hired thugs still standing, the Sofas and two more who had not been trampled at the mine. The five men ran past Moxie's house and into town. They had no choice about where to go because the side streets were blocked with furniture or cars or lines of people. Fires burned, their flames lighting the horses and their riders in red as they herded Spells and his men down the high street. Huge horse shadows leapt about the road and the buildings, as if all the Marchogion Rhydd there had ever been were here on this night too.

Noel and his gang had parked their rusty bangers across the street. Spells had run into a dead end. Animals and humans united in their rejection of this man, this creature who had done so much harm. Everyone was there, but there was no sign of any of Moxie's family.

Moxie leapt from Melys' back, with Rhiannon close beside her. They ran to where Noel and half a dozen others held Spells and his thugs fast.

'Punch him in the throat, Moxie,' Noel said. 'We'll hold him for you.'

She wanted to, but she wanted something more.

'Where are they? Where are my family?'

'Who are you?' Spells snarled.

Noel pulled Spells' yellow hair, which came off in his hand.

'Her name's Moxie. Show her some respect or I'll take off more than your wig.'

Moxie looked to Rhiannon, standing grim faced beside her. 'I'm her grandchild, and we're your worst bloody nightmare, Spells,' Moxie told him. 'So where are they?'

He laughed then – a horrible laugh. 'Oops, I think I might have left the gas on.'

Up the hill at the mine, there was a huge explosion. Spells looked at Rhiannon.

'Torched all your kids now, girly,' Spells said. 'And your niece and grandson!'

Half the town raced up the hill with Moxie and Rhiannon, but the heat coming from the front of the mine was too great to even get close. Someone let off a fire extinguisher into the flames, but it was like sticking plaster on a severed leg. Rhiannon was literally tearing at her hair.

'Round the side,' Moxie yelled. 'The other door.'

They raced between the broken walls and knots of bramble and found the door through which Spells had escaped. Smoke was coming from it, but no flames. Moxie pulled her T-shirt over her nose and mouth and ran inside. Rhiannon did the same. The smoke and heat were terrible, but Rhiannon's head torch cut through the murk.

'Door!' Moxie said, pointing. It was just an office door, locked, but no match for two determined women who wanted to kick it down. Steph, Marianne and Non were on the floor behind it, unconscious but otherwise OK. In the smoke, Moxie made out other people coming in to help. They'd help Rhiannon get the women out. Now she had to find Ryan and Kuhyen.

There was a spiral staircase at the back of the room, lit with flames coming from the room above. Moxie groped her way up. Flames licked across the wall beside her, but she could still see two small bodies at the far end of the room – Ryan and Kuhyen, tied to a table. Moxie pulled the steak knife from her belt, much more useful for this kind of thing than a sword, and cut them free. But the smoke had got to her. She was swaying on her feet. How would she carry both of them? She didn't have to make a choice. Just as her knees gave way, Dyl was suddenly beside her.

He got them out, all three of them, and laid them on the grass. Moxie thought the sound of

Ryan coughing his guts up was one of the best sounds she'd ever heard because it showed he was alive. She tried to get up, but Dyl's hand gently pushed her down.

'He's fine,' Dyl said. 'And so's the little girl. Your gran's got it in hand. And the ambulance is coming, and the police.'

Moxie knew she must be dead or dreaming. *Ambulance? Police?* 'How d'you get 'em to come here?'

Dyl smiled at her. 'They took a bit of convincing but they listened to me in the end,' he said. 'Spells was big enough bait to get them off the bypass for a change.'

Then Dyl, her Da, took her hand and said, 'Just relax now, Moxie, OK? Let someone else take the strain for a minute, eh?'

16. Epilogue

Kuhyen's letter had arrived at the house on Cemetery Street. It was, everyone agreed, little short of a miracle, as post was pretty hit and miss these days. But perhaps it was a sign that things were looking up. She didn't say much, a lot of 'thank yous', but the photograph she sent said it all.

'Digger,' Ryan said, and pointed to the beloved toy that he had insisted Kuhyen take home to Vietnam.

'Look at that!' Rhiannon said when she saw it. 'Just like the picture she did on my house wall. Family and animals. Nobody needs any more than that, do they?'

No, Moxie thought, they didn't. Even though her family was not like the ones in stories, but was cracked up with tragedy; even though it was made of people who were dodgy, like ex-cons turned police informers and party girls who were off with the fairies; even though her mam was really her aunty and she and her brother had different mothers; even though their family pet wasn't a waggy dog but a knobbly old horse. Moxie decided that her family was piebald, a mix of darkness and light, and that's what gave it a strength and a magic that perfect families would never even understand.

Quick Reads

Quick Reads offer a series of short, engaging books which appeal to all tastes and reading abilities for the price of £1 each, encouraging less confident readers to pick up a book. These titles are aimed at adults who find reading a struggle or who've lost the habit of reading, and are also perfect for readers who are short of time. The initiative is coordinated in Wales by the Books Council of Wales and supported by the Welsh Government.